PONY CAMP diaries

Megan and Mischief

tiger tales

5 River Road, Suite 128, Wilton, CT 06897
Published in the United States 2018
Originally published in Great Britain in 2006
by the Little Tiger Group
Text copyright © 2006, 2018 Kelly McKain
Illustrations copyright © 2006 Mandy Stanley
ISBN-13: 978-1-68010-424-0
ISBN-10: 1-68010-424-1
Printed in China
STP/1800/0183/0218
10 9 8 7 6 5 4 3 2 1

For more insight and activities, visit us at www.tigertalesbooks.com

PONY CAMP
diaries

Megan and Mischief

by Kelly McKain

Illustrated by Mandy Stanley

tiger tales

For Millie (star rider!), Jody (star mom!),
and the whole Wallington crew.

With thanks to Jodie Maile (star instructor!) for getting
me back in the saddle and for her invaluable help
and advice with this book.

And special thanks to Rose and Prince,
and Janet Rising (star consultant!)

THIS DIARY BELONGS TO

MEGAN
★ THE ★
BRAVE!

Contents

Dear Riders,

A warm welcome to Sunnyside Stables!

Sunnyside is our home, and for the next week it will be yours, too! We're a big family—my husband, Johnny, and I have two children, Olivia and Tyler, plus two dogs ... and all the ponies, of course!

We have friendly yard staff and a very talented instructor, Sally, to help you get the most out of your week. If you have any worries or questions about anything at all, just ask. We're here to help, and we want your vacation to be as enjoyable as possible—so don't be shy!

As you know, you will have a pony to take care of as your own for the week. Your pony can't wait to meet you and start having fun! During your stay, you'll be caring for your pony, improving your riding, enjoying long rides in the country, learning new skills, and making friends.

And this week's special activity is a breathtaking beach ride. Just imagine you and your pony cantering across the sand together! Add swimming, games, movies, barbecues, and a gymkhana, and you're in for a fun-filled vacation to remember!

This special Pony Camp Diary is for you to fill with all your vacation memories. We hope you'll write all about your adventures here at Sunnyside Stables—because we know you're going to have a lot of them!

Wishing you a wonderful time with us!

Jess xx

Monday, 9:16 a.m.

Wow! I'm actually here at Pony Camp! At last!
Jess, who runs Sunnyside Stables, gave me this
fabulous Pony Camp diary to write down my
adventures this week. There's even a space on
the cover to put a picture of MY pony—I can't
wait to meet him … or her! I wonder who I'll
get! Mom and Dad got me here mega early
and no one else has come yet, so I'm starting
right this second! Jess gave me a map, too, and
a timetable, and we're having a gymkhana
on Friday with prizes and everything—
SO exciting!! I've never entered any
competitions before, and I'd love to win
a rosette for my pony bulletin board at
home. That would be awesome!

When Mom and Dad were registering me
in the office, which is in the yard, I took a peek
around, and this place is amazing!

I saw a really huge horse in the stables, the kind that pulls plows. I hope I don't get him 'cos he's enormous!

There were these two cute ponies tied up in the yard, too, getting their tails washed by a girl with curly blond hair, but they'd be too small for me. Then I noticed a huge field up the track that had a lot more ponies in it, including a cute piebald and a prancing palomino. I can't wait to find out which one will be mine!

I'm so nervous, it feels like my breakfast cereal is doing a dance in my stomach!

I've never stayed away from home on my own before, and I'm extra jittery 'cos of this secret thing I did. On the registration form, in the comments section, I put that I would like a forward-going pony!

This is a big deal because at my riding school,

I always end up with the slow ones. I'm too shy to say anything, though, so people think I like lumbering along at the back of the ride, having to use my legs like crazy just to get a tiny trot. But I'm ready for a challenge now—and Pony Camp is it! No one knows me here, so I'm going to be a different girl. Not Megan who still has a night-light on in the hall and won't join in the soccer game at recess because she's afraid she'll get whacked in the head by accident. But a whole new kind of Megan....

I'm even hoping to do some more jumping while I'm here (I've only done it a couple of times so far).

I'm lying on my bunk bed writing this.

I've claimed the bottom one which is cool 'cos you can hang your towel down from the bed above and it makes a secret camp. I've already hidden my backpack under my bed in case we get to have a midnight feast! I can't wait to meet the girls I'm sharing my room with. And most of all, I can't wait to see which pony I'm getting!

Oh, gotta go, some of the other girls are here now…. (I really hope they like me!)

P.S. I just met my roommates, Olivia and Gabrielle. Olivia is Jess's daughter and she lives here all the time (how lucky is that?!) and she has her own pony named Blaze (how even luckier is that?!). Gabrielle is really nice, too (phew!). She has these cool ponytail holders, and me and Olivia just helped her braid her long, wavy blond hair, and it looks really cool. I'm going to buy the exact same ones the second I get home.

Gabrielle's ponytail holders

Still Monday,
after a yummy lunch

I GOT MY PONY!!

His name is Mischief, and he's absolutely
beautiful. Here's a quick profile of him:

U Megan's Pony Profile

star

NAME: Mischief

HEIGHT: 13 hands (hh)

AGE: 6

BREED: Arab cross

COLOR: Palomino

socks

MARKINGS: Star and stripe, and white socks on hind legs

FAVE FOODS: Pony nuts and carrots

PERSONALITY: Really sweet, but a bit mischievous
   (I'll write more about that later!)

♥ Pony Camp Diaries ♥

Before we got our ponies, Jess did a welcome talk and introduced us to all the staff. Lydia is the girl with curly blond hair who I saw before. She's a stable hand, which is my dream job – imagine getting paid to take care of ponies all day! Sally is the instructor, and she has these cool army print half chaps that I've wanted since I saw them in *Pony* magazine. Jess takes care of us and does all the cooking (we're all going to help, too, but she's in charge), and her husband, Jason, is the Yard Manager and Olivia's dad!

Next, Jess had us say our names and where we were from. There are nine of us including Olivia, three in each room. Cassie is

the youngest (she's only six), and she's in with
Chloe and Tina, two friends who came all the
way from Madison! In the other room there
are three almost-teenagers—Kate and Karen
the twins are smiley and nice, but Jade looks a
bit moody. She wears a lot of make-up and has
blond hair that she keeps flicking around as if
she's in a shampoo ad.

Anyway, back to MY PONY!

When Lydia led this beautiful pony out of
the stable, I crossed my fingers really tight,
hoping he was for me. Then I heard Sally
say, "Megan, you asked for a challenge,
so we'll try you on Mischief."

I could hardly believe it! He was the stunning palomino I'd seen in the field! I wanted to jump up and down and scream, "Yes! Yes! Yes!" but I didn't in case it spooked the ponies.

Kate got this handsome black gelding named Rusty.

Gabrielle got the cute piebald whose name is Prince.

Moody Jade got a glossy chestnut named Chance, who flicks her tail around in the

same way Jade does with her hair—so they're perfect for each other! I don't remember who the others got because I was too excited about Mischief!

We tacked up (Lydia helped me with getting the bit in) and waited to mount up on the block, ready for our first lesson. Once I was

on, I felt so high up on Mischief, but since he's
a light build, I could wrap my legs around his
sides nicely. I even tightened my own girth, and
I felt really cool and grown up just figuring it
out myself—until Mischief started wandering
off while I still had my leg forward. Lydia had to
come back over and hold him still, so then
I didn't feel very cool after all!

At first, when we got in the manège, we
just had to walk around on the track and think
about sitting up straight and keeping our hands
relaxed and our heels down. There were no
complete beginners and everyone could trot at
least, so that was okay.

Then it all went not okay, 'cos Mischief
started doing Mischievous Things. Like:

Mischievous Thing 1
We did trotting to the back of the ride one by
one, and I think Mischief got bored of walking

around and around waiting for his turn because
he kept going really close to the person in front,
which was Gabby, and almost sticking his nose
up Prince's tail. Sally told me to use half halts to
keep him in check, but that didn't really work
because he just kept stopping completely!

Mischievous Thing 2

When it was our turn and I asked for trot,
Mischief just leaped backward and started
skittering around. Everyone was looking at me
and I felt really panicky, but then Sally strode
toward us, and Mischief started behaving after
all. Well, until…

Mischievous Thing 3

When we did some practice of going over
trotting poles, Mischief got a little excited and
barged up the side of Chance. I pulled on the
reins and leaned back, but I still crashed legs with

Moody Jade. I'm sure it didn't hurt, but she made
a big deal about it, crying, "Argh!" really loudly
and saying that I had no control. I pretended not
to hear, but I just KNOW everyone else was
listening. After that I tried really hard to keep out
of trouble, but...

Mischievous Thing 4

We were going around cones and
Mischief went absolutely miles
around them, like way over to

the edge of the manège. Sally called out, "Time
to take charge and get tough, Megan!" which
was awful because it was like being scolded in
front of everyone, and I was already trying my
hardest—but Mischief was just ignoring me!

But the worst thing was when Sally asked
some of us to ride our ponies into the middle
(including me!) while the others had a canter

23

around the track. I was really upset because I'd done a lot of cantering on Lucky back home, even if it was only short bursts after a lot of time spent encouraging him.

I'm worried that Sally thinks I'm not a very good rider. I really want to win something in the gymkhana and take another shot at jumping. But for that to happen, I'll have to get tough with Mischief like she said. But HELP! How do I do that? I'm not the sort of person who usually gets tough about anything. Usually I tell Dad and he gets tough for me, like when Julian Mason put a snowball down my back at school and Dad called Mr. Thomas, the principal. But Dad isn't here to help me now! I'll just have to turn into Megan the Brave and show Mischief who's

Oh, time to go again!

Still Monday (just!)

Olivia lent me her flashlight, so I'm writing this in
bed after lights out!

I'm so exhausted—we've done so much
already, and it's only the first day.

After our lessons we had a lecture
on grooming, and I found out what the
different currycombs are for. (I'm not one
of the girls who helps out in the yard where
I ride at home, so I don't know much
about grooming.) Then we had a snack and
swam in the pool for our Evening Activity. Me,
Olivia, and Gabrielle were doing synchronized
swimming—well, trying to anyway, and we
ended up in total hysterics. I'm so lucky to have
such great roommates! And Olivia is so lucky to
live here all the time!

Gabrielle is in the bunk above me, so I'm
scribbling this really quietly 'cos she's fast asleep.

Currycomb

She has an iPod and before dinner, she let me listen on one of the earphones, even though they're the little ones you stick right in your ears and she could have been grossed out and not wanted me to share it!

Well, Mischief did three more Mischievous Things this afternoon, including almost making me fall off when we were riding without stirrups by skittering around when Lydia pushed a wheelbarrow past. I tried really hard to be Megan the Brave, but I felt like crying when we dismounted. Gabrielle gave me a hug and Olivia said, "Don't worry! It can be hard getting used to a new pony, and Mischief isn't called Mischief for nothing!"

Best friends!

♘ Megan and Mischief ♘

I said, "But everyone thinks I'm awful!" and
Olivia said, "No one thinks that." But I think
she was just being nice 'cos we both heard Jade
giggling when I lost my balance. At that moment
I suddenly missed Mom and Dad so much.

Sally called me over when we were
untacking and asked if I wanted to
switch to this other pony named Star,
who is very reliable. I know reliable
means slow, as in another plodder.
I could feel myself almost starting to
cry, but I managed to hold it in and say I
wanted to stick with Mischief.

STAR - reliable but
probably another
plodder!!

Sally said, "Okay, that's fine for now, but I'll
just have to keep an eye on how things go.
I want you to get the most out of your week
here, Megan, and I'm sure you do, too."

Wow! I can't believe she asked me to switch.
I will have to get tougher if I want to keep my
handsome Mischief—and quickly!

27

After the Grooming Lecture we did the Practical Learning, which meant fully grooming our ponies from head to hoof. Lydia came around to help us, and I got to try out the plastic currycomb to lift the mud and grease out of Mischief's coat. When I was brushing around his shoulder with the dandy brush he nuzzled up to me, so I think he loves me, too!

I even secretly pretended that he was my very own pony and that we'd come here for a vacation together, with him in a horse trailer.

I can't wait for tomorrow because we get to go to the yard right after breakfast and do jobs like real pony owners! I'm going up to the field with the other girls whose ponies live out to catch them and bring them down to the yard.

I didn't call Mom and Dad tonight even though we had the choice after dinner because I was still a little upset about my bad lesson and I didn't want Mom to worry (which she does a lot). I'll make a new start tomorrow and prove to everyone that I can handle Mischief, and then I'll have something great to tell them both on the phone!

Night night,
sleep tight!
Sweet pony dreams
'til morning light!

Tuesday 11:00 a.m.,
before the beach ride

Oh! I fell asleep last night after writing in my diary, so we didn't get to have a midnight feast. Hopefully we will tonight!

Right now it's morning break and everyone's getting ready to go on the beach ride, so I'm quickly writing this. I have had such a fantastic time this morning with my wonderful Mischief!

This is what we did:

8:20 a.m.

Brought in the ponies. We also did a quick bit of grooming and picked out their feet. Mischief had a big stone near his frog so I had to be very gentle and careful.

♡ Megan and Mischief ♡

9:00 a.m., breakfast time

This was cool because there are a lot of little boxes of cereals to choose from and you can have any kind you want, or even mix two kinds together. I had two of my favorites, which I'm not usually allowed because of all the sugar.

9:30 a.m.

Usually we would get our ponies ready for the first lesson, but it's different today because we're going on the beach ride! So instead we had our lecture, which was on how to do bandaging and put on boots. This is really important for traveling because if you bandage up your pony's tail, it won't rub while he's in the horse trailer. And putting on boots or bandages keeps his legs from getting bumped if there's a sudden jolt or slamming of brakes!

First Lydia did a demonstration on her bay, Shy, and then we all took a turn on our ponies. We're only taking four to the beach (Blaze, Rusty, Twinkle, and Mischief—yippee!) but we practiced on our own ponies anyway. Lydia showed us how to tie them up on the yard safely, and then how to put a bale of straw between you and your pony's hind legs just in case they spook and kick backward (not that Mischief would ever kick me because he is my beautiful wonder horse!). My tail bandage went a little wrong at first, and it all unraveled halfway and hung down like streamers.

I did it wrong!

But Lydia showed me that I could start it off tight around the dock without hurting Mischief and then it held together better (although it still wasn't perfect).

Still not perfect!

Then we got to lead the beach-ride ponies
up the track to the horse trailers. On the way
I secretly pretended that Mischief was my own
pony again and that we were going back to
the horse trailer to go home together. I got so
excited watching Jason and Lydia load them up.
I've never ridden on the beach before, and Olivia
says it's really fun. I've got to go now because
she's saving the back seat of her dad's truck for
me and her and Gabrielle, even though everyone
else has to go in the bus!

Two minutes later!

Oh, no—my happy mood is ruined!

I'm writing this in the back of the truck because we're still waiting for everyone else to pile into the bus. As I was walking over to the truck, I spotted Moody Jade throwing a fit because Chance isn't going to the beach and she has to ride Rusty after Kate instead.

I wanted to try and make friends with her after the leg-crashing thing, so I tried to be nice by saying, "Don't worry, Jade, it's only for one ride." But she just sneered at me and said, "What do you know? Your pony's coming with us, which is so not fair, especially when you can't even handle him properly!"

I just stood there staring at her with my legs shaking and my eyes filling up with tears. And then she did this really mean "What are you staring at?" look.

34

WHAT ARE YOU STARING AT?

Olivia just this minute read this and said, "Don't let her spoil your trip," and she's right.

In fact, I'm just going to keep out of her way from now on.

Before dinner,
back from the beach!

WOW! The beach ride was amazing! I was in the first group with Olivia and Chloe. Kate was supposed to be riding with us, too, as Rusty is her pony, but Jade made such a fuss that Kate let her go first (boo!).

We were on a private beach that the owners let Sunnyside use, so there were no people around. While we tacked up, Sally warned Jade not to ride too close to the ocean because Rusty doesn't like the water. Jade just huffed and said, "Well, then, why couldn't we bring Chance instead?" Sally just smiled and said, "Come on, cheer up and try to enjoy yourself," which just made Jade look even more grumpy.

GRUMPALUMP

♘ Megan and Mischief ♘

As soon as we mounted, I felt really nervous because I've never even gone riding outside my pony school before. I kept thinking that Mischief might just suddenly take off down the beach, but Lydia spotted me looking scared and came and held on to him. I wasn't embarrassed at all—just glad!

Then we were off! Sally rode at the back on her own horse, Blue, and Olivia was at the front on Blaze. Lydia rode Shy along beside us—she had a lead rope clipped to her D ring, which made me feel really safe. We walked on for a while, getting used to the sand, which felt softer than the wood chips in the manège. Then we moved into a trot. It was so awesome jogging along in sitting trot and when we went rising I wasn't thinking "up, down, up, down" like usual but just sort of doing it. Mischief had a lot of impulsion, and I only had to lightly squeeze my lower leg against him, so it was much easier than normal for me to keep it all together and not flail around. And it wasn't scary at all—it was fantastic! I wasn't worried about hitting the fences at the sides like I am in the manège. And we didn't have to do any turns or try to stay on a track; we just had to go forward, so I felt much more like Megan the Brave than Megan the Terrified. Olivia was right about beach rides. It was AweSOME!

ME TODAY!
Megan the BRAVE!

◡ Megan and Mischief ◡

Sally said my new confidence showed in my seat and hands, and that's why Mischief was listening to me, and I couldn't help smiling. We went back to walk then, and Sally corrected our positions and ran through the aids for going into canter, just as a reminder. We picked up rising trot again, and when she gave the word we went sitting and asked for canter. Olivia and Blaze were off like a rocket, then Rusty and Jade, and then me and Mischief! I tried to sit still and not throw my body forward, which is my number one bad habit, and for once I just kept my seat and went with the rhythm and it felt like we were flying!

I don't know if I should write about what happened next, in case Jade somehow finds out and starts not liking me even more, but this is my diary and I want to put what truly happened so here goes. As we cantered up the beach, Jade kept nudging Rusty over into the waves, so

Sally called, "Jade, stay on the sand, please. I've already told you Rusty doesn't like the water."

But Jade didn't listen and just rode closer and closer to the ocean. Just as Sally said crossly, "Okay, and easing back into trot, everyone," this wave broke on Rusty and he sort of leaped backward and Jade lost her stirrup.

Then just as she was trying to get it back, Rusty went back into trot really quickly and Jade lunged forward, clinging to his neck. She probably could have sat up, except then he dropped his head and snorted loudly, and she toppled off into the ocean! It was so funny because it looked like Rusty had dumped her there on purpose.

(Maybe he had!)

Olivia and I couldn't help laughing!

But Jade was NOT finding it funny! Instead she was rolling around, clutching her leg and groaning. As Sally dismounted and checked her out, I stopped laughing and started to worry that she'd seriously hurt herself. But Sally said, "You're fine, just a bit wet, that's all. I did warn you not to go near the water."

"I didn't!" grumped Jade. "It was Rusty's fault!" But Sally just raised one eyebrow and said, "Let's not argue about it. You're okay, and that's the main thing."

Sally gave Jade a leg up but she was still grumbling about the fall. I forgot not to look at her so she did the "What are you staring at?" face to me again, and I quickly turned away and started talking to Olivia. But it really made my stomach churn because I can't stand it if someone doesn't like me. We just walked and trotted on the way back, and even though Jade was still grumbling, she rode on the exact bit of sand that Sally told her to and not a single inch closer to the water.

When we got back to the picnic place, everyone wanted to know why Jade was dripping wet. She was really snappy and wouldn't tell them, so while Jess helped her to dry off, Olivia explained about the fall. Everyone laughed and Moody Jade got even moodier.

I didn't join in the laughing, hoping she'd notice, but she just flounced off around the back of the horse trailer to change into the dry stuff Jess had brought "just in case."

⊃ Megan and Mischief ⊂

Then the second group got ready to ride.
I held on to Mischief while Gabrielle mounted,
and I kept giving her all these tips about being
confident and relaxed with him and sitting up tall,
but she just smiled and said, "Megan, chill, I'll be
fine!"

Kate was on Rusty and when Sally warned
her about the water thing she laughed and said,
"Don't worry—there's no way I'm going near
the ocean, not after what happened to Jade!"
That made everyone start laughing again, which
made Moody Jade even more angry.

I watched Gabrielle heading off on Mischief
and I only felt a tiny bit jealous! Then we had our
picnic lunch, with cheese and tomato or tuna
and cucumber sandwiches. I had one of each
without picking out the cucumber or the tomato.
Eating what I'm given is part of me being Megan
the Brave, instead of Megan the
Fussy like I am at home.

After that, Chloe got her model horses out, and we all played with them (except Moody Jade, who read a magazine and ignored us). We made up a whole game about running the only riding school in the Sahara Desert, and we even shaped some of the sand and pebbles into a jumping course! I chose the palomino, of course, and pretended that it was Mischief and that I was riding him over these really high jumps and winning tons of rosettes.

On the way home in the truck, Gabrielle told me that she'd had fun on Mischief, but she wished Prince had gone on the trip instead and she said she couldn't wait to get back and see him. I was secretly glad because I don't want anyone else to start loving Mischief when he's MINE!

In bed, in the dark with
Olivia's flashlight!

I'm waiting for midnight so we can have our
secret feast! We all made a pact to stay up until
exactly 12 o'clock, but it's only ten past ten
and Olivia and Gabrielle are both fast asleep.
Still, I don't mind waiting by myself because
I've got a lot to write. At midnight I'm going to
wake them up so we can have the rest of my
candy and the strawberry licorice that Gabrielle
brought, and talk about ponies and maybe even
tell ghost stories. Olivia says she knows a great
one about a headless horseman (eek!).

Well, I did call Mom and Dad tonight, and I told them all about how well the beach ride went and how happy Sally was with my riding. Mom got a little worried about us cantering on the beach, and I had to convince her that it was all perfectly safe and that I had my body protector on and my chin strap done up and long sleeves and my proper boots and everything.

My stomach churned up a bit when I put the phone down, like it did when Jade pulled her "What are you staring at?" face at me on the beach. I've hardly thought about Mom and Dad since I've been here, but speaking to them made me miss them so much.

I cheered up during the Evening Activity, though, which was a ping pong tournament. Olivia was a star and me and Gabrielle weren't very good, but it didn't matter because it was so much fun!

Olivia's dad pretended to be joining in just
because he was the adult who had to organize
us, but we could tell he had practiced a lot and
was really trying to win. Karen beat him in the
final, though, and we all cheered, and she won
a cool pony pencil case with all new things in it.

It's only the second day of Pony Camp
and I've already learned about bandaging and
grooming and been cantering on the beach,
and made some completely awesome friends
and met Mischief, my star pony—this really is a
dream vacation!

Oh, I just yawned a huge yawn. Maybe I'll
close my eyes for a minute or two….

Wednesday morning

I can't believe we all slept straight through midnight—again! Today is really exciting because we're learning the games we'll be playing in the gymkhana on Friday. Well, some people know them already so it's just practice for them, but I don't! There was this one gymkhana at our stable that I was going to be in, but at the last minute I got scared and wimped out and just ended up watching with Mom. But this time, I am going to do it!

I'm really looking forward to riding Mischief after we did so well yesterday on the beach. He came straight up to the gate this morning and let me put on his halter and lead rope without any problems at all. I'm sure everything will go great from now on and Sally will see that I'm a good rider, and Jade will be AMAZED and start liking me.

After the lesson

Ugh. I've had the worst morning ever. I'm trying really hard not to cry, but my hand is shaking like crazy. The others are having their break downstairs, but I didn't feel like eating anything so I'm lying on my bed writing this.

Things started off okay-ish with the relay race. I'm really getting a better position in canter now, although I still couldn't turn smoothly at the top, so I lost a lot of ground for the way back. But when we were doing the egg-and-spoon race I had to put both reins in one hand, and Mischief suddenly swerved off his track and ran across the other ponies' lanes for no reason. Jade got angry with me because she had to slow Chance down to keep from crashing into us. When I finally managed to halt she shouted, "If you can't control that pony, you shouldn't be on it!"

49

Even though she made me feel really shaky, I
knew I had to defend Mischief. "Mischief is not
an 'it', he's a 'he,'" I said, trying not to let my
voice wobble. "And anyway, ponies
are unpredictable. You can't always
tell what they'll do."

Jade made that huffing sound she always
does and said, "Don't blame that monster for
your mistakes!" Then she turned Chance and
trotted back to the start line, her egg perfectly
balanced on her spoon.

Ugh! How dare she call Mischief a monster!
I rode back to the starting line, too, still grumbling,
and Olivia said, "Don't worry about her. She's
just really moody. It's nothing personal."

But I think it IS personal. Jade doesn't seem to
pick on anyone else. Why is it always me?
I was upset about Jade for the rest of the lesson,
so I wasn't very brave for the other races, like
the apple bobbing and the bending. And when

we practiced the Chase Me Charlie, I was only half concentrating because I was trying to avoid Jade's eye, so I got knocked out on the first hole. Also, in a lot of the races we had to turn when we reached the far end of the manège and then canter back, and I just couldn't get it right. Mischief kept going along on the track, like in a normal lesson, and the harder I tried to ask him around, the more wrong it seemed to go. Sally kept telling me to relax my hands and use more leg, but I just couldn't get it together. So then she told me to put the reins in one hand and hold on to the pommel if I felt unsteady. That's what you do when you're just beginning!

I really want Mom and Dad to be proud of me on Friday at the gymkhana, but at this rate I'm never going to win anything!

After we'd dismounted, Sally called me over
for a "chat." Except it wasn't really a chat 'cos
I let her do all the talking. I knew if I opened
my mouth to say anything I'd start crying.
Sally explained that she might have to switch
me off Mischief for the rest of the week. She
said, "Megan, it's very difficult for you to enjoy
yourself or learn new skills when you're having
such basic problems with control."

She doesn't understand that it's not just
about the riding. Mischief is my pony, and I love
him so much that I couldn't stand for us to be
apart. And I am enjoying myself, mostly. All the
grooming and tacking up is so much fun, and
the beach ride was amazing. But when I opened
my mouth to say that to Sally, nothing came out
except "but I love him!" in a teary, croaky voice.

Sally said more softly, "I'll have to talk to
Jason and Jess about it, and I'll let you know
after lunch, okay?"

All I could do was nod, but inside my thoughts were racing. What will the others think if I get taken off Mischief? What will Jade say? Will Mischief think I don't love him anymore?

Oh, Olivia's calling up the stairs for me. At least we have our Stable Management lecture next, about feeds and pony health, so I can do my Practical Learning with Mischief. He's definitely mine until after lunch and I want to spend every second I can with him, before the worst might happen.

Afternoon—in our bedroom

I'm writing this while I'm waiting for the others to come back from their afternoon ride. I didn't go, which is a long story, but I'll try to write it all down in here before Olivia and Gabrielle get back.

Well, I felt really sick with a tummy ache after lunch—it must have been the fish sticks. Gabrielle and Olivia tried to take my mind off it, but then it got worse, so Jess suggested I lie down. I went and cuddled up on my bed with Olivia's black Labrador, Cooper, and tried not to think about Sally's decision.

Olivia came to get me just before the hack, but I still didn't feel well, so she went down and told Sally and Sally said I could miss it.

☽ Megan and Mischief ☽

When everyone had gone, Jess came in
and sat down on the bed, and asked if I was
feeling any better. I started off talking about my
stomachache and ended up telling her about
the disaster-filled gymkhana practice, and how
Sally might take me off Mischief.

Jess smiled in a kind way. "Sally told me,"
she said. "And I wonder if you're not feeling
well because you're worried about Sally's
decision."

I realized then that while it was mainly the
fish sticks, it might have been the worry, too,
just a little bit. I nodded, and then I suddenly
blurted out, "Sally thinks I'm terrible."

Jess said, "Megan, that's nonsense. If you're
not learning and improving, then it's our fault for
putting you on the wrong pony. We just want
you to enjoy yourself."

"But I enjoy myself on Mischief!" I cried.

Jess gave me a look like she wasn't sure.

I said, "Well, maybe it's not exactly fun in the manège when he's acting up, but it was awesome on the beach and I just love having him as my pony and grooming him and taking care of him and…." I felt myself almost start crying then. I really, REALLY didn't want to lose Mischief. "It just feels as if he's mine," I sniffled.

Jess nodded. "Well, Megan, maybe we can do something about this. In the end it's Sally's decision, of course, but perhaps…. Get your boots on and meet me in the yard by Mischief's stable in five minutes." Then she stood up and bustled out of the door.

By a lucky coincidence I didn't feel sick anymore, so I went to the bathroom and washed my face, then went down to the porch, grabbed my helmet, and pulled on my boots. I poked my head around Mischief's stable door and there was Jess, tacking him up. She passed the girth to me and asked, "What's the thing you're having the most difficulty with?"

"Everything," I grumbled, lifting the saddle flap and buckling it up.

"Well, let's just choose one thing to start with," she said, and even though I couldn't see her face, I could hear in her voice that she was smiling. "If Mischief knows you're going to keep trying until you get something right, it'll make everything else easier, too, because you'll have more confidence. And he'll know you mean business."

"Okay," I said, thinking quickly. "Can we work on turning a circle, because it was my worst thing this morning, so it's probably sticking in Sally's memory right now!"

Once we got into the manège, Mischief and I warmed up on both reins and rode a few circles in walk. Then we got to work, and Jess explained that my outside leg controls the shape of the circle and my inside leg controls the size. She said I shouldn't think about turning more tightly, but more smoothly instead and she even gave me a schooling stick to gently tap Mischief with if he ignored my leg aids. Every time Mischief tried to fall in, Jess called, "Keep going, Megan! Leg! Leg! Leg!"

Well, I was giving it so much inside leg I thought my leg might actually fall off, but it still didn't work. I pulled hard on my outside rein to try and bring Mischief back on track, but all that happened was that his head twisted around and his body stayed where it was.

"Relax!" called Jess. "You're so busy yanking those reins you've forgotten about your seat and legs. If you turn it into a battle of wills, I think we know who'll win!"

So I tried to relax my hands and concentrate on keeping a good leg and seat position.

It didn't work at first, and Mischief still kept falling in and leaning on me, but I was determined not to give up. Jess called, "Sit up tall and look where you're meant to be going, rather than where you're afraid Mischief will actually

go!" This made me laugh and then Jess laughed, too, and I started to feel a little better. Jess was right—when I started acting like the boss, Mischief did stop being so mischievous.

Pretty soon I'd gotten the hang of riding a circle in trot from the A marker to the center point and back around, without it looking triangle-shaped. I even managed to do some figure eights to C!

"You see," said Jess. "You can do it!"

Then we practiced cantering up to the end of the manège and the turn to come back again, like in the gymkhana games. Jess showed me how to make my turns tighter by using my body weight. At first it felt like just another complicated thing to remember, but then I started to get the idea. Jess was delighted, and said we should stop there on a high note and that I'd done really well. By the end I felt so happy, and I made a big deal over Mischief, too, to show him what a good boy he is.

V. clever HORSE!

I could tell he was happy, too, by the way he snorted and nuzzled up to me when I was leading him out of the manège.

Before today I couldn't understand it when Mischief ignored me, but now I know it's up to me to be clear in whatever I'm asking and not give up asking for it, and then everything works much better! With all Jess's help this afternoon I secretly think I might have a chance in the gymkhana—not to come first, but maybe to get a third or something.

Back in the yard, I got up the courage to ask Jess the BIG QUESTION, which was

WILL I HAVE TO SWAP PONIES?

Jess sighed. "You know that's not up to me, Megan," she said. "But hopefully with what we've done today, you'll have improved enough to get more out of riding Mischief."

Yay! So *she* thinks we
should stay together at least!

Jess let me tie Mischief up in
the yard and groom him, with Lydia supervising
me while she skipped out the surrounding
stables and refilled the water buckets. When I
was cleaning around Mischief's eyes with the
pink sponge, I told him how well he'd done,
and how much I love him. He sort of nodded
his head down and blinked at me, so I know
for sure now that he loves me, too. Then I
had to explain the bad news that we might get
separated. I could tell he was sad about that, so
I gave him a big hug. But I also said that because
of our good teamwork today we might be able
to stay together, and he cheered up a tiny bit.

I can hear hooves in the yard—I'll go and
help the others untack and turn out the
ponies—and tell Olivia and Gabrielle what
happened this afternoon!

It's Thursday,
and I've just woken up (yawn)

Well, the softball game last night was fun—Tina
turned out to be a great batter and Karen
scored a lot for our team—but I was still mainly
thinking about Mischief and whether we will
be split up. We played in the field next door to
where the ponies live, so when I was fielding
I went really deep so I could watch Mischief
chomping the grass.

Me, Olivia, and Gabrielle didn't have a midnight feast last night—again!—even though I was actually still awake at exactly 12 o'clock. I decided not to wake them up because I was having a nice daydream (are they still called daydreams if you have them at night?) about Mischief and me rescuing a sheep that had fallen down a ditch.

I was also too busy being nervous about what Sally will decide. Now the moment is here and I've got to go down to the yard and find out the news....

9:00 a.m.,
just before breakfast

Sally said I could stay on Mischief! Yes!
Yes! Yes! And phew! Phew! Phew!

The exact thing she said was, "Jess is also
a qualified instructor, and if she feels you've
improved enough to keep riding Mischief, then
that's fine with me, but you must keep up the
good work and stay in control."

I said, "Yes, absolutely, I promise," and then
I hurried straight over to Mischief's stable and
told him the news. I gave him a big hug, and I
could tell he was as happy as me by the way he
nuzzled my neck. Yippee!

Mischief

Megan

It's especially great because today we're all going on a picnic ride. We're having our lecture right after breakfast and then getting our horses ready and we'll be out from about 11:30 until 3:30 in the afternoon, and we'll have our lunch out in the countryside, too, which is the picnic part! That is just so

COOL!

I can't wait!

And I'm going to show Moody Jade just what a fantastic team Mischief and me are, too. Everything is perfect again! Now I've got to go and pick out which cereals to mix this morning.

Morning break

Oh, no—things have gone really wrong because I've had a fight with Olivia and Gabrielle.

We were eating our oranges and cookies before we set off on the picnic ride, and I was sitting next to Olivia and kind of staring into space and thinking about whether Mom might get me the army print half chaps. (I left the magazine on the kitchen table open to the ad as a hint.) Then Jade came up and said, "You look nervous, Megan. I don't blame you. There's no way you'll be able to handle Mischief on the picnic ride."

"I'm not worried about anything," I said, determined not to get upset. "Am I, Olivia?"

I expected Olivia to say, "Of course not," or something like that, but instead she just shrugged and looked at the table. "Well, I'm not," I mumbled. "Just because people are

67

staring into space thinking about half chaps, it doesn't mean they're worried."

Jade gave me a mean look and walked off, saying, "Well, you'd better not slow us up."

Just then, Gabrielle came over and asked Olivia if she could ask Jess for more chocolate cookies because there were only vanilla frosted left on the plate, and before I could stop myself I pointed at Olivia and blurted out, "She thinks I'm not good enough to ride Mischief on the hack out!"

"I didn't say that!" Olivia cried.

"But you didn't stick up for me when Jade said those things!" I challenged. I don't really know why I was so annoyed with her. I just was.

"Well, to be honest, I am a little worried about you," Olivia admitted. "The picnic ride isn't the same as on the beach, Megan, where you can just point forward and wander along."

"What! I do NOT wander!" I cried.

"Okay, sorry, wrong word," said Olivia, "but what I mean is, there are gates to open and you have to make sure Mischief doesn't barge through. And you need good control for the canters, or you'll end up dragged through a hedge at the top of the field. And there might be cows that you have to stay calm around or you'll get Mischief all nervous and…."

Maybe what Olivia was saying made sense, but all I heard was, "You're not good enough to ride Mischief, and by the way you're not good enough to ride Mischief, and, oh, did I mention that you're not good enough to ride Mischief?"

"What do you think, Gabby?" I asked.

Gabrielle blushed bright red and looked at her feet. "Well, I guess you should listen to Olivia," she mumbled. "I mean, she's been on a lot of these rides before and…."

"Is Olivia a trained riding instructor?" I shouted. "If Sally and Jess both think I can do it, then that should be fine with Olivia, shouldn't it? Just because she has her own pony and she gets to live here all the time doesn't mean she knows everything, does it?"

Olivia glared at me as if she was about to shout back, but then she turned to Gabrielle, saying, "But you can see I'm only saying it because she's my friend, can't you?"

Even Gabrielle got angry then. "I don't know!" she cried. "I only wanted a chocolate cookie, and now you two are putting me in the middle! In fact, I think I'll go and talk to Chloe and Cassie and Tina instead!"

And with that she marched off, and me and Olivia glared at each other, and then *she* marched off, too. That was when I spotted Jade looking at me with a smug kind of smile on her face—she'd seen the whole thing. So now Gabrielle is ignoring Olivia and me, and the two of us are ignoring each other. I feel really upset about it and I can't believe that my so-called friends could be so mean. So far they haven't come over here, and there's no way I'm going up to either of them. After all, it's their fault we had a fight, not mine.

I know Jade's still watching me sitting here on my own, so I'm pretending to concentrate really hard on writing this. I don't want her to do that "What are you staring at?" face at me again.
I will just have to be Megan the Brave and have a fantastic picnic ride on Mischief and prove everyone wrong—so there!

Thursday, after the ride

It's after dinner, and we're all in the living room watching this movie called *Spirit*, with yummy hot chocolate and popcorn. I have the DVD at home and I've seen it about 23 times, so I'm writing this instead. It's very dark in here, so it's hard to keep my writing in a straight line. The movie is instead of our Evening Activity, which was meant to be swimming and a barbecue, but there's a thunderstorm outside, so we can't go in the pool. I'm secretly glad because I'm really worn out from the picnic ride and all the terror and excitement that happened to me on it.

So here is the story….

MEGAN THE BRAVE!

We started our picnic ride with Sally riding in front and Jason bringing up the back to make sure we were all safe. It was good because we had to go down the road a little bit before cutting up on to a path, so we got to use our road safety skills that we did in our lecture this morning, like riding on the edge where we could, keeping together as a group, and thanking drivers who come past slowly (well, driver, because there was only one). We all had these bright yellow vests over our jackets so we were visible, too.

I was nervous at first, because after what Jade had said this morning, I didn't want one single little thing to go wrong, but it was awesome riding Mischief out in the countryside, and he was really listening to me. But I did feel sad that me and Olivia and Gabrielle were still not talking. Olivia was in the back, chatting to her dad, and Gabrielle was riding with the younger girls. I didn't feel like I could talk to Kate and Karen since Moody Jade was with them, so I had to ride by myself.

Me on my own

Sally must have noticed because she called
for me to trot up to the front of the ride and
chat with her. Unlike before when I was too
upset to say anything, this time we talked a lot.
She said she was really proud of me for giving
it my all with Mischief, and she also said how
much improvement she could see. I said thanks
and how I liked her jacket, because I wanted to
say something nice back. We stopped talking
after a while, and it was good just riding along
beside each other. Mischief was a little over-
enthusiastic on some of the trots we did, but
I remembered to use my half halts to get him
listening and responding to me.

There were some fallen branches and little shrubby things on this grassy bank, and Sally let the older girls and Olivia and Cassie take a turn at jumping over them. I even got to jump over a log with Mischief! When Sally said we'd reach the picnic site soon, I could hardly believe it. It felt like no time had gone by, but my bottom was getting sore, so I could tell it had.

There was a nice, gentle, uphill-sloping track at the edge of a field of corn, and Sally said we could canter to the top (everyone can canter now). It was great, flying up the hill with the sound of pounding hooves all around. But then suddenly Mischief was going faster and faster, and then he broke into a gallop! As we left the rest of the ride behind us, I panicked and lost my left stirrup. I was desperately trying to get it back and at the same time thinking

HELP!

♞ Megan and Mischief ♞

For a few seconds I forgot everything I ever knew about riding. My hands went flying everywhere, and my bottom was bouncing around, and I just clung to Mischief's mane for dear life. Then finally I caught my breath and managed to struggle up to sitting. I gathered the reins, pulled back sharply, and shouted, "Whoa!" but Mischief didn't listen. Trying not to panic, I focused on getting my stirrup back, hoping that would give me more control. It took a few tries, but then I got it. I glanced backward and saw that everyone else was miles behind.

While I was busy panicking, Mischief veered off the track and started galloping across the field instead. Suddenly the hedge into the next field was looming up ahead of me. It felt a hundred times scarier than racing up to the edge of the manège in the gymkhana games practice, and I had no idea how I could make Mischief stop when he was going so fast!

Well, the answer is that I didn't. He jumped the hedge! Then we were galloping across the next field and I was leaning back and pulling the reins with all my strength and shouting, "Whoa!" as loud as I could, but he still wasn't stopping. Writing it now, it sounds like a long time, but it all went by in a complete flash, and I hardly had time to think.

Me and Mischief, very scary!

The hedge I jumped!!

That's when I heard galloping behind me—it was Sally and Olivia. Sally kept calling, "Turn him, turn him!" and I tried but nothing happened, and I started to really panic as the next hedge appeared on the horizon. "Megan, turn him NOW!" Sally shouted. "I know you can do it! Come on!"

☾ Megan and Mischief ☾

I was just panicking by then and thinking, *I
can't, I can't!* when Olivia yelled, "There's a road
on the other side of that hedge!"

That really made me listen. I was the rider and
I was meant to be in charge, and I couldn't let
Mischief get into danger.

"Come on, I know you can do it!" Olivia was
shouting.

Suddenly I remembered the things Jess had
said when we were practicing circles and turns.
I adjusted my position, took a deep breath, and
pulled on my right rein, squeezing hard with my
left leg. The hedge was really close now, and I
felt like just shutting my eyes and hoping for the
best, but I knew I couldn't give up. I kept my seat
and told Mischief to turn. "Come on, Mischief!"
I cried. "We're a team! Just turn for me!" The
hedge got closer and closer and then … he
turned! It was so sharp that I lost my stirrup
again, but I didn't care.

"Now circle him!" Sally called. "Nice and tight. And use your half halts. That'll slow him down."

Even though it felt like my shoulders were being pulled out of their sockets, I brought him around into a circle. We went around and around and around, and it seemed to go on forever.

Just when I was so scared and tired that I felt like leaping off, Mischief dropped into canter, and then trot, and finally came to a halt. I let the reins go slack with relief, and just like that he dropped his head and started eating the grass, as if nothing had happened.

That's when I noticed the rest of the ride standing by the gate—they'd seen everything!

I hardly dared to look at Sally—I thought she'd be furious with me! But she just said, "Wow, Megan. That was Amazing!"

♘ Megan and Mischief ♘

I must have given her a really confused look because she added, "The way you stayed focused and regained control! Just staying on would have been impressive, but you managed to slow him right down, without getting dragged through that hedge!"

"Do you really think he would have jumped it and gone into the road?" I asked.

Sally laughed. "Oh, no, I don't think so. That one's much higher than the last. But saying that, with our Mischief you never can tell. Let's just say I'm very glad you handled him well and we didn't have to find out!"

Then she said, "Okay, let's get back on track. We're not even supposed to be going this way!"

And, signaling for us to follow, she turned and trotted back toward the group by the fence.

Me and Olivia looked at each other and both started talking at once. I was saying, "You were right, I couldn't handle Mischief out here," and Olivia was saying, "You were great. You handled him really well. I'm sorry."

Then we steered up close to each other and tried to hug to make up, which was pretty funny because we had to lean really far over. Sally called out, "Come on, you two, stop horsing around! There's a picnic waiting for us!" and everyone laughed. When we got back to the group, Gabrielle wanted to make up, too, so now we're all friends again.

Best friends
AGAIN!

Megan and Mischief

When Jess arrived in the truck with the picnic, everyone was talking about how brave I was. (I'm not saying that to boast, but it's true, and I did promise to write down everything that happens at Sunnyside!) They kept telling her braver and braver versions of what happened, until it sounded like Mischief had been bucking and rearing and half-jumping the hedge, and I'd stopped him just by using my little finger.

Then Jade said really loudly to Karen, "She was just showing off, making him gallop like that—it's a miracle she stayed on. She can't even handle him in the manège, let alone out here!"

Everyone turned and looked at me, and Gabrielle started saying, "That's not true!" but I was so annoyed that I just stood up for myself without thinking. "Of course I didn't make him do it on purpose!" I shouted. "Unlike you forcing poor Rusty to go near the water. And at least I stayed on even at a gallop, when you fell off in trot!"

Everyone laughed then, remembering what happened to Jade at the beach. We were staring hard at each other and I was holding my breath, wondering what awful thing she'd say next. But Jade just looked away and I thought, *Wow, I really stood up for myself.* Maybe I can be Megan the Brave with girls, too, and not just ponies!

★ MEGAN THE BRAVE! ★

When Jess gave me my sandwich and chips, she winked at me and I winked back—we both knew the secret of how I could turn Mischief and how I could keep him on a circle!

Oh, I'm going to stop writing in my journal now and watch *Spirit* because my favorite part is coming up!

Friday—our last day—boo!

Well, we finally had a midnight feast! Olivia
told us the headless horseman story, and it
ended with her going "YOU!" really loudly
and making us jump and scream. We had to
quickly pretend to be asleep after that because
Jess heard the noise and came around with
a flashlight, but then we got up again and ate
the strawberry licorice and said everything in
whispers.

We had to pack up our stuff this morning
after breakfast, so we're all ready to go home
right after the gymkhana, because our
parents are coming to cheer us on.
I'm so excited, and I'm going to try
my hardest to win a rosette.

I'm still a little worried about Jade spoiling
things for me, because she hasn't talked to me
or even looked at me since I stood up to her.

What if she's planning to do something mean to me at the gymkhana, like running around with her bright pink jacket flapping open to spook Mischief or swapping my egg-and-spoon race egg for one that's not hard-boiled so that it goes all over me?

I'm probably just letting my imagination get the best of me—but still, I wish I knew what she's thinking.

U Megan and Mischief U

Friday afternoon

The gymkhana starts in 15 minutes, and all the parents are arriving now. We're supposed to be getting our final things packed, but I did mine really fast so I could do some writing!

Mischief looks so handsome! We had a wonderful time getting ready for the show after lunch, with our ponies tied up in the yard so we could groom them in the sunshine. I didn't even think a single thought about Jade or what she was doing or whether she was thinking about me. I was too busy getting ready for the gymkhana.

Here are all the things I did:

1. First, we all brought our tack out to the picnic benches, and gave everything a really good clean and polish.

2. I gave Mischief a really good groom, including wiping his bottom parts with the

special T sponge (ugh!).

3. I polished his coat with a damp cloth and some conditioning spray until it was really glossy.

4. I combed his mane until it was all smooth and shiny.

5. I tried to braid his tail and weave ribbons into it, too, but I messed it up, so Lydia showed me how I could just tie some different ribbons around it instead, and that looked really nice.

6. I borrowed some of Olivia's hoof oil to make Mischief's hooves really shiny. Gabrielle lent me some sequins, too, but just when I was about to stick them on, Mischief leaned down to my ear and I knew he was trying to tell me he didn't want to wear them! So I gave the sequins back to Gabrielle and said no thanks.

7. I got into my last set of clean riding stuff, which I'd been saving especially for today, and Gabrielle put my hair in a low ponytail

with ribbons that matched the ones around Mischief's tail.

Even if I don't win any of the races, maybe I will have a chance of winning something in the tack and turnout comp. Mischief certainly deserves it—I think he's the most handsome pony in the world!

STILL Friday afternoon

I am writing this in the car on the way home, because I couldn't wait one single second longer. I'll begin where I left off so I don't forget anything.

When we were all ready for the gymkhana, we took pictures of each other, so I have a ton of photos of Mischief and me, and some great ones of Olivia, Gabrielle, and me, too. Then Jess took some of the entire group together, using each of our phones, so we had to keep smiling for what felt like FOREVER. Then—

Oh, I can't tell things in order—I just have to write down the best parts now! Me and Mischief won two rosettes! We got third place for tack and turnout and also … first place for the bending race!

♘ Megan and Mischief ♘

Everything Sally and Jess had taught me about circles and turns really came in useful going around those cones, plus the accidental practice I had on the picnic ride, of course! I was neck and neck with Jade and it was really close, and before I became Megan the Brave I probably would have let her win to try and make her like me. But not today! I urged Mischief on with my legs and voice, and he seemed to understand my determination and just stepped up the pace a little bit more (without galloping this time, thank goodness). I could hardly believe it when I cantered back over the finishing poles before anyone else.

Olivia and Gabrielle, and Mom and Dad, and Jess and Sally went crazy cheering for me. I was so happy that I didn't even wonder whether Jade was angry about me winning!

We had a ton of fun in the other games, too, and I didn't care one bit that Mischief did some excited bucks in the egg-and-spoon race and my egg went flying off to who knows where!

In the Chase Me Charlie, I actually got up to the fourth hole before knocking the pole down. Sally shouted, "Oh, Megan, you can jump higher than that!" and everyone who had been on the picnic ride laughed. I knew she was only joking, though, and I was really happy with getting that far—I'm definitely going to work on my jumping back at my riding school.

When I went up for winning the bending race at the award ceremony, Sally handed me my rosette and said, "You need speed and control for that race, and you and Mischief certainly have both now. Great job!" She shook my hand and Mom was clapping like crazy, and Dad was snapping away with his camera.

♡ Megan and Mischief ♡

Mom said later that even though her heart was in her throat (her exact words) watching me do the races, she couldn't believe how confident I'd become. I was going to tell her about what happened on the picnic ride, but I've decided to wait until she reads this pony diary—she's probably had enough excitement for one day. And she had a present waiting for me in the car, too—the army print half chaps! I gave her a big hug and said, "But how did you know I'd win a race?"

Mom laughed. "They're not for winning, Megan!" she said. "They're for having the courage to go on vacation all on your own."

That's when I realized I was already a little brave to start with, to come here without knowing anyone, and to make new friends, and try new things, like beach riding and sandwiches with weird things in them.

Maybe Megan the Brave was somewhere inside me all along, but hidden!

MEGAN ☆ THE ☆ BRAVE!

I was just heading to the house to get my stuff when Jade came up to me. I thought she might be about to say something mean, but she just held out her hand. Before I could think about I was doing, my hand was shaking hers. "I'm sorry for being weird with you before," she said. "And great job winning the bending race."

"It's okay," I mumbled. "And great job in the apple bobbing."

94

♘ Megan and Mischief ♘

I don't know what changed her mind about me. Maybe she realized I'd stopped caring what she thought, or maybe she just wanted to try on my army print half chaps, but I didn't worry about it. We girls all said good-bye to each other with lots of hugs, and me and Olivia and Gabrielle all swapped e-mail addresses and promised to keep in touch. Then I had to say good-bye to the one person (well, pony!) I would miss most of all—my Mischief.

While the parents all had a cup of coffee with Jess and Sally, Lydia and Jason supervised us in the yard. I led Mischief back to his stable and untacked him, and took out his tail ribbons.

I spent a long time untying them so we could have as much time together as possible. While I was giving him lots of love and attention, I whispered in his ear that even if I rode, say, 22 more ponies in my life, I would never forget him and he'd always be my favorite. That was when he nuzzled my neck in a way that said, "Even though different kids ride me at Pony Camp each week, you'll always be my favorite, too!"

☾ Megan and Mischief ☾

Finally, I could hear Dad calling that it was time to go. I gave Mischief one last hug. I felt a little sad, but mostly I was happy because I had gotten to meet him in the first place, and because he taught me to be brave. Even though my week at Sunnyside is over, I'll have my memories forever—and this diary, of course!

When I go back to my riding school next week, I'm going to keep on being Megan the Brave and ask to go on Dancer or even super-fast Duke. Well, maybe I'm not ready for him just yet, but one thing's for sure—no more plodders for me!

PONY CAMP
diaries

Learn all about
the world of ponies!

◦⌒ Glossary ⌒◦

Bending—directing the horse to ride correctly around a curve

Bit—the piece of metal that goes inside the horse's mouth. Part of the bridle.

Chase Me Charlie—a show jumping game where the jumps get higher and higher

Currycomb—a comb with rows of metal teeth used to clean (to curry) a pony's coat

Dandy brush—a brush with hard bristles that removes the dirt, hair, and any other debris stirred up from the currycomb

Frog—the triangular soft part on the underside of the horse's hoof. It's very important to clean around it with a hoof pick.

Girth—the band attached to the saddle and buckled around the horse's barrel to keep the saddle in place

Grooming—the daily cleaning and caring for the horse to keep it healthy and make it beautiful for competitions. A full grooming includes brushing its coat, mane, and tail and picking out the hooves.

Gymkhana—a fun event full of races and other competitions

Hands—a way to measure the height of a horse

Glossary

Mane—the long hair on the back of a horse's neck. Perfect for braiding!

Manège—an enclosed training area for horses and their riders

Numnah—a piece of material that lies under the saddle and stops it from rubbing against the horse's back

Paces—a horse has four main paces, each made up of an evenly repeated sequence of steps. From slowest to quickest, these are the walk, trot, canter, and gallop.

Plodder—a slow, reliable horse

Pommel—the raised part at the front of the saddle

Pony—a horse under 14.2 hands in height

Rosette—a rose-shaped decoration with ribbons awarded as a prize! Usually, a certain color matches the place you come in during the competition.

Stirrups—foot supports attached to the sides of a horse's saddle

Tack—the main pieces of the horse's equipment, including the saddle and bridle. Tacking up a horse means getting it ready for riding.

Pony Colors

*Ponies come in all **colors**. These are some of the most common!*

Bay—Bay ponies have rich brown bodies and black manes, tails, and legs.

Black—A true black pony will have no brown hairs, and the black can be so pure that it looks a bit blue!

Chestnut—Chestnut ponies have reddish-brown coats that vary from light to dark red with no black points.

Dun—A dun pony has a sandy-colored body, with a black mane, tail, and legs.

Gray—Gray ponies come in a range of color varieties, including dapple gray, steel gray, and rose gray. They all have black skin with white, gray, or black hair on top.

Palomino—Palominos have a sandy-colored body with a white or cream mane and tail. Their coats can range from pale yellow to bright gold!

Piebald—Piebald ponies have a mixture of black-and-white patches—like a cow!

Skewbald—Skewbald ponies have patches of white and brown.

Pony Markings

*As well as the main body color, many ponies also have white **markings** on their faces and legs!*

On the legs:

Socks—run up above the fetlock but lower than the knee. The fetlock is the joint several inches above the hoof.

Stockings—extend to at least the bottom of the horse's knee, sometimes higher

On the face:

Blaze—a wide, straight stripe down the face from in between the eyes to the muzzle

Snip—a white marking on the horse's muzzle, between the nostrils

Star—a white marking between the eyes

Stripe—the same as a blaze but narrower

White/bald face—a very wide blaze that goes out past the eyes, making most of the horse's face look white!

Fan-tack-stic Cleaning Tips!

*Get your **tack** shining in no time with these top tips!*

- Clean your tack after every use, if you can. Otherwise, make sure you at least rinse the bit under running water and wash off any mud or sweat from your girth after each ride.
- The main things you will need are:
  - bars of saddle soap
  - a soft cloth
  - a sponge
  - a bottle of leather conditioner
- As you clean your bit, check that it has no sharp edges and isn't too worn.
- Use a bridle hook or saddle horse to hold your bridle and saddle as you clean them. If you don't have a saddle horse, you can hang a blanket over a gate. Avoid hanging your bridle on a single hook or nail because the leather might crack!

- Make sure you look carefully at the bridle before undoing it so that you know how to put it back together!
- Use the conditioner to polish the leather of the bridle and saddle and make them sparkle!
- Check under your numnah before you clean it. If the dirt isn't evenly spread on both sides, you might not be sitting evenly as you ride.
- Polish your metalwork occasionally. Cover the leather parts around it with a cloth and only polish the rings—not the mouthpiece, because that would taste horrible!

⸎ Grooming Time! ⸎

*Find out how much you know about
caring for your pony with this fun quiz!*

1. The first thing to do when grooming is:
   a. Brush your pony's tail.
   b. Apply hoof oil.
   c. Pick out your pony's hooves.

**2. The most important reasons to groom
your pony are:**
   a. To take a break from mucking out, to
      clean, and to bond.
   b. There's only one—to clean!
   c. To bond, to check for injuries, and to
      clean.

3. You should groom your pony:
   a. Every week.
   b. Every day.
   c. Every two days.

**4. The only brush you should use on
your pony's face is a:**
   a. Body brush.
   b. Metal currycomb.
   c. Plastic currycomb.

5. When grooming, your brush strokes should be:
   a. Long and firm.
   b. Quick and soft.
   c. Slow and cautious.

6. To clean mud off your pony, the best thing to use is a:
   a. Cactus cloth.
   b. Dandy brush.
   c. Body brush.

7. To clean the body brush when grooming your pony:
   a. Draw it along a metal currycomb after several strokes, then tap the currycomb on the ground.
   b. Rinse it in your pony's water bucket.
   c. Wipe it on your jodhpurs after every few strokes.

8. Your pony's mane should never be brushed with a:
   a. Mane comb.
   b. Body brush.
   c. Plastic currycomb.

Beautiful Braids!

Follow this step-by-step guide to give your pony a perfect tail braid!

1. Start at the very top of the tail and take two thin bunches of hair from either side, braiding them into a strand in the center.

2. Continue to pull in bunches from either side and braid down the center of the tail.

3. Keep braiding like this, making sure you're pulling the hair tightly to keep the braid from unraveling!

4. When you reach the end of the dock—where the bone ends—stop taking in bunches from the side but keep braiding downward until you run out of hair.

5. Fasten with a braid band!

Gymkhana Ready!

Get your pony looking spectacular for the gymkhana with these grooming ideas!

A running MANE BRAID

Ribbons on her brow band

Matching ribbons in tail braid

POLISHED Coat

HOOF oil & Sequins on hooves

Turn the page for a sneak peek
at the next story in the series!

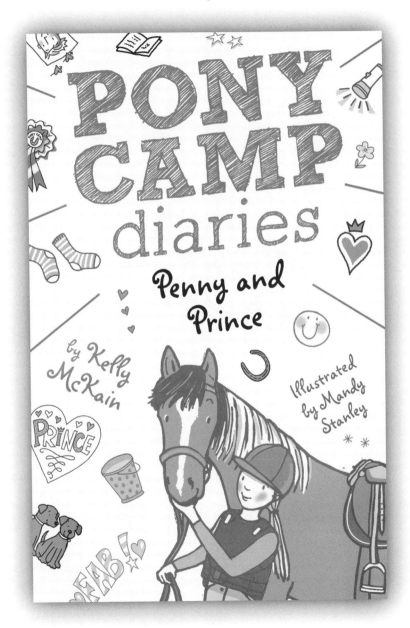

PONY CAMP diaries

Penny and Prince

by Kelly McKain

Illustrated by Mandy Stanley

PRINCE

FAB!

Monday, at Pony Camp!

Jess has just given me this special diary to write down all my adventures at Sunnyside Stables. I'm so glad to be here! It looks like such a great place—and I'm really excited about riding for the first time in weeks. On the way in I saw a field full of beautiful ponies, and I couldn't help trying to guess which one will be mine! But I'm also feeling very nervous because I don't know if I'll even dare to get on her (or him!).

That's because two months ago I had a fall at my local riding school. They were holding a show jumping competition, and I'd entered the novice class on my favorite pony, Pepper. I went clear in the first round, and I really wanted to win, but in round two I got my strides wrong and jumped the combination a little long. Pepper clipped the second set of poles and almost fell over—and I went flying off and smacked right into the wing, and then landed strangely on my arm. When I got up, it was hanging at a funny angle—turns out it was broken! It should have really hurt, but at the time I couldn't feel anything. Mom said later it was probably because of the shock. When the pain did come, it was terrible. Two paramedics made me a sling and helped me out of the manège, and then Mom took me to the hospital. I didn't get back on Pepper that day, of course. And my arm took six weeks to heal.

But the fall isn't really the problem (my arm's fine now)—it's what it has done to my confidence. I did try to have a lesson at my stables last week, to get used to things again, but I didn't even manage to get on. I just couldn't make myself do it. It was awful because all the helpers, Hailey (my instructor), and Mom were standing there saying encouraging things, but I was really dizzy and shaky. In the end I ran off to the bathroom, pretending I was going to be sick. And then I stayed in there for a long time, just feeling so silly and embarrassed, until Mom banged on the door and took me home.

Right now, I'm sitting on a bench outside the office, which is next to the tack room. There are stables around all three sides of the yard, and a handsome (and massive) carthorse is peering out at me! It's really cool here because there's a swimming pool (I love swimming) and also these sweet black Labs named Buster and Cooper, who gave me big, sloppy kisses when I arrived! So even if I don't dare to ride this week, I'm sure I can help out in the yard and play with the dogs and go swimming—so I'll still have fun. Just hanging around here will be fantastic, and maybe the pony I'm given for the week will help me get back in the saddle again!

I know I shouldn't eavesdrop, but I'm desperately trying to hear what's going on in the office, because Mom said she would have a word with Sally and Jess about me losing my confidence. I feel squirmy with embarrassment about her telling them, but I'm also relieved because if they know, they can help me get back to riding. But—ugh!—I just had a horrible thought. What if they say, "Oh, yes, yes, we understand" to Mom, and then when she's gone they get angry with me if I get scared and don't want to do things? And what if I can't get back on and the other girls all laugh?

Oh, it's just so annoying that this has happened! I wish I could

SNAP OUT OF IT...

but I can't.

But maybe it will be easier here because no one knows what I was like before the fall. It's weird to think that I've got a stack of rosettes at home, for show jumping competitions and dressage tests and one-day events. Nothing scared me!

But there's no way I'm telling anyone here that, because then they'll expect me to be really good. And right now, I'll be happy if I can just *sit* on a pony!

This nice girl, Lydia, just asked me if I want to help her pick out Dallas the carthorse's giant feet. If everyone here is as nice as she is, I should be fine. So no more being scared—I've decided that Sunnyside is the perfect place for me to get back in the saddle. I'm going to get on—today!

Still Monday,
before the first lesson (gulp!)

My new roommates have gone down to the yard, but I'm hanging around up here to quickly write what's happened so far.

When everyone came out of the office, Sally spotted me helping out with Dallas and gave me a big smile. "Don't worry, Penny, we'll get you riding again," she said. So she's nice, too—phew! I asked her not to tell anyone else about the fall or about me being so nervous now, and she promised she wouldn't—thank goodness. I don't want anyone feeling sorry for me.

The other girls all started arriving then, so I thanked Lydia for letting me do Dallas's feet and followed the crowd upstairs. I'm sharing a room with this girl Jennifer, who has light brown hair with curled-up ends. Her suitcase is huge—I think she brought everything she owns!

Our room is actually Olivia's own bedroom (Olivia is Jess's daughter), and it's really nice of her to share it with us. Olivia has her regular bed by the window, and me and Jennifer are in the bunk beds. I said I didn't mind which one I had, so Jennifer chose the top one. (I was secretly hoping for that one, too, but making friends is more important!)

They both seem nice, especially Olivia, but I think I might have a BIG problem keeping my fall a secret.

When we were unpacking, I kept glancing at Olivia and thinking, *I KNOW that girl.* And then suddenly, I figured it out. We both competed in a local show jumping competition—and I beat her! From the second I realized, I was just desperately hoping she wouldn't recognize me, but she soon said, "Haven't I met you before, Penny?"

I wouldn't usually lie, but I didn't know what to do, and I found myself saying, "Um, no, I don't think so."

Olivia said, "Well then, you've got a twin out there who beat me and Tally at the Watertown show!"

I made myself grin and reply, "Really? That's SPOOKY."

Luckily we got distracted by Jennifer telling us all about her last show jumping competition and reenacting her fabulous victory. It sounded amazing (almost too amazing to be true, actually). Then she said she could canter a circle on the spot in dressage and Olivia instantly cried, "No way! I don't believe that's possible even if you are really, really good unless you're a grown-up professional with a specially trained horse and everything!"

Jennifer looked kind of surprised and embarrassed at the same time. She mumbled, "Well, I haven't actually DONE it yet, but I read about it in my magazine, and I figure I could do it with some practice."

"Yeah, right!" Olivia scoffed. She's so pony-crazy that she can spot a fib a mile away. Ugh! I hope she doesn't spot mine!

Jennifer was a little huffy after that. She turned to me and demanded, "So, what have YOU done?" I just completely panicked and blurted out, "Oh, you know, the usual." Then I added, "Hey, I love your fleece," to change the subject.

But Jennifer kept at it, asking, "But like what, though?"

I went all red and flustered then, like I do in math when I've been daydreaming and Mr. Ramirez asks me a question. I kept unpacking and mumbled, "Um, walk and trot, obviously, some canter, and a little jumping."

"Oh," she said, "so you're—"

$16\% \text{ of } 100 = ?$
$3/4 + \frac{1}{2} = ?$
$75 + 21 = ?$

"But only a tiny bit of jumping—pole work, mainly," I added quickly, in case she started asking about heights and combinations and all that.

Jennifer just gave me an unimpressed look and turned back to her bulging suitcase. Phew! I think I got away with it! Of course, I wanted to reveal the truth and shout, "Actually, I'm the girl from the Watertown show, and I've even done cross country and a Pony Club team dressage competition—so there!" But I kept quiet.

Me at the Watertown show where I beat Olivia and Tally!

Oh, Jess is calling me down to the yard now. Time to meet my pony (hooray!) and see if I dare ride again.

Help!

If you love animals, check out these series, too!

Pet Rescue Adventures

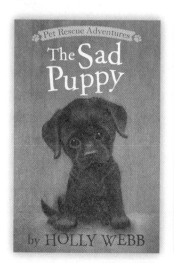

Pet Rescue Adventures
The Sad Puppy
by HOLLY WEBB

Pet Rescue Adventures
A Kitten Named Tiger
by HOLLY WEBB

Pet Rescue Adventures
The Homeless Kitten
by HOLLY WEBB

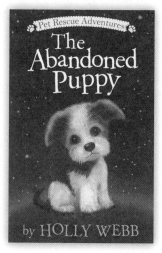

Pet Rescue Adventures
The Abandoned Puppy
by HOLLY WEBB

ANIMAL
+RESCUE CENTER

ANIMAL
+RESCUE CENTER

The Abandoned Hamster

by TINA NOLAN

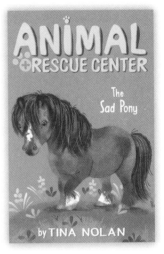

ANIMAL
+RESCUE CENTER

The Sad Pony

by TINA NOLAN

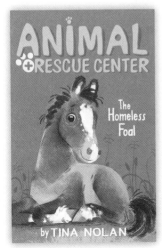

ANIMAL
+RESCUE CENTER

The Homeless Foal

by TINA NOLAN

ANIMAL
+RESCUE CENTER

The Porch Puppy

by TINA NOLAN

Kelly McKain

Kelly McKain is a best-selling children's and YA author with more than 40 books published in more than 20 languages. She lives in the beautiful Surrey Heath area of the UK with her family and loves horses, dancing, yoga, singing, walking, and being in nature. She came up with the idea for the Pony Camp Diaries while she was helping young riders at a summer camp, just like the one at Sunnyside Stables! She enjoys hanging out at the Holistic Horse and Pony Center, where she plays with and rides cute Smartie and practices her natural horsemanship skills with the Quantum Savvy group. Her dream is to do some bareback, bridleless jumping like New Zealand Free Riding ace Alycia Burton, but she has a ways to go yet!